CANNIBALS!

A story of Sawney Bean

by

Helen Welsh

rooshie doo

Published by Gallus Publications,
PO Box 29055,
Dunfermline KY11 4YL

Cover design by Liam Doherty, with original artwork by Kirsty Richards
(front cover) and Stuart Steedman (back cover), both of Commercial Primary
School, Dunfermline. Illustrations by Frank McCormick.

The right of Helen Welsh to be identified as the author of this work has been
asserted in accordance with the Copyright, Designs and Patents Act 1988.

ISBN 0-9546625-5-5

A catalogue record for this book is available from the British Library.

Printed and bound by Printing Services (Scotland) Ltd., Broomhead Drive,
Dunfermline.

Author's acknowledgements

I am grateful to Ron Deen for his excellent and well-researched pamphlet on the Sawney Bean story. I would also like to thank Bridget Donald for inspiration regarding youth work; and George Welsh for preventing me falling off the cliff at Ballantrae.

Helen Welsh, Dunfermline, July 2004

CHAPTER ONE

Five pairs of adult eyes are resting on Alex, who shifts uncomfortably in his seat. He can feel their pity; but he doesn't want it. How dare they pity him? If only his mother were here. There's a silence and he feels they're expecting him to say something, but he doesn't know what to say, so stays silent.

The adults crack before he does, as he knew they would. The Panel Chairperson leans forward and speaks to him gently: 'You do understand that we're doing this for your own good, don't you, Alex?' He says nothing but glares at the chairperson, who continues: 'Your mother is not able to look after you at the moment, and you don't have anyone else who can step in and take her place. The local authority has a duty to look after you in these situations.'

1

'I can look after myself,' Alex growled.

'No, I'm afraid you can't.' And the chairperson turned to the social worker. 'Mr. Jamieson, you have carers lined up?'

Andy Jamieson spoke up: 'Mr. and Mrs. Duffy are very experienced foster carers and they live within a mile of the hospital where Alex's mother is staying. They have a good understanding of mental health problems, and will make sure Alex gets to visit his mother regularly. They live on a bus route which passes Alex's school, so he won't need to change schools. Even if Mrs. Bean's stay in hospital is extended, Mr. and Mrs. Duffy will be able to keep Alex, so there won't be any need for changes in residence.'

'And will Mrs. Bean consent to this arrangement?'

'I'm afraid she isn't in a position to consent right now.'

'Ah. In that case we need to be looking at compulsory rather than voluntary measures of care.'

'Yes, that is what I recommend.'

Alex was furious. They were talking about him as if he wasn't even there. He spoke out loudly: 'I'm not going.' He noticed the impact his words had on the adults; they looked nervous, their eyes flickered back and forwards to the door of the Hearings room, as if they expected him to dash off out of there. He wondered for a moment whether he should do just that. He was a good runner, he'd be out of there in a flash. But the Reporter would probably ring an emergency bell and the doorman would catch him on the way out, and there would be humiliating struggle which would just result in him being dragged back in again, looking stupid. Better to wait his chance.

The panel member to the right of the chairperson

leaned forward and spoke to him across the big table: 'I have met Mr. and Mrs. Duffy and they are very nice people. I'm sure you'll like it there.' Alex looked at her with scorn. As if it was just about liking people! Alex could get on with anybody if he wanted, he wasn't worried about going to strangers, at least not all that worried. It was just that they were doing it against his will. He squirmed with frustration that he couldn't control his own life. Why wasn't his mother here? Surely she could have lasted out another day before getting herself admitted to hospital? It would have made such a difference; they'd have given her another chance.

But there was nothing else for it; the adults made the arrangements, pronouncing him to be in need of compulsory looking after by the local authority, and that was it; he and Andy Jamieson were walking down John Street towards the car park, with Alex now officially a Child In Care.

But on their way to the foster carers' home, Andy got a call; then another and another. It seemed all the foster carers in Scotland were full up.

After each call Andy was getting more and more – what? Alex tried to put his finger on it. Irritated? Embarrassed? Desperate? It seemed they couldn't find a place to put Alex. Finally a place was found, but Alex could tell it wasn't ideal. 'What?' he heard Andy say, 'you're joking of course. What about council policy? And where is it anyway? That's no use. It can't possibly be the only place... Well look I'm really not happy about this, I can't discuss it just now but I'll be putting in a strong complaint...'

Alex's heart was sinking. He wondered what his

mother was doing right now; whether he might still make a run for it, and find her, and bring her home, and make everything normal again. He felt a few tears at the edge of his eyelids and blinked them away. Andy was speaking to him. 'Well Alex, son, we've got a place for you but it's not what I had in mind.'

'What?'

'It's a children's home – I know I said it's against policy for children your age, but it seems all the foster placements are full up. It'll only be temporary, I'll get something better sorted out within a few days. But right now, I'm afraid that's all that's on offer.'

Alex was silent. A children's home. Well, that couldn't be all that bad could it? A bit of company; maybe not have to answer so many adult questions when there were plenty other kids around.

'It's quite a long way away.'

'So what about school?'

'You'll have to go to the local school.'

'What, just for a few days while you find something else?'

'Well, maybe not tomorrow, there'll be stuff to do... it'll depend how long you're there I suppose... but soon you'll have to go to school.'

'What about visiting my mum?'

'I'll fix it.' By now Andy had pulled a road atlas from the back seat and was searching for the right page. He showed Alex where they were going: 'Here – on the coast, quite far down. Ballantrae.'

'Ballantrae.' Alex said nothing else for a while, as Andy found the route and steered the old blue Ford in the right direction. Alex had heard of Ballantrae before, but he couldn't quite place it. Andy put the radio on and let Alex choose the station; they both disappeared into their own thoughts under the shelter of the pop music. The road went on, and on, and on, and it began to get dark. When they passed through a town called Girvan and saw the first road sign to Ballantrae, Alex remembered where he'd heard of the place before; his grandfather used to talk about it, before he died. 'Son,' he used to say, 'Stay away fae Ballantrae.' Alex had never asked why.

CHAPTER TWO

By the time they got to the Home, Alex was feeling queasy, and dozing. It was the long and winding road that did it, with the sea pounding away on the right hand side. Darkness fell about eight o'clock and they arrived twenty minutes later. Andy missed it in the dark, and Alex woke up as the car was reversing. 'Are we nearly there?' he asked.

'I think that's it – can you read that sign from here?' Andy was peering at a small bronze plaque on a stone pillar by an iron gate. Alex had excellent eyesight: he read it out: 'Seaview South Ayrshire Council Please Ring and Wait'. There was a metal ring in the gatepost; Andy pulled it but they couldn't hear anything; he pulled again twice and lights went on in the porch up the drive. A female voice shouted 'coming, coming!' and suddenly a whole crowd materialised. Various shapes, sizes, genders, and dress styles. Alex gazed in confusion but Andy raised a hand in salute to a small roundish woman in the centre of the crowd. She smiled back, first at Andy then at Alex. 'So you got here,' she observed, 'Hi. I'm Alice. You'll be Alex?'

Alex nodded. So who was Alice, he wondered. Surely too young for staff? Alice answered his unspoken question with another puzzle: 'I'll be your key worker,' she said. Key? Worker? Fortunately Andy did the speaking for him, and sorted it out so that they found their way through the staring crowd and into an office sort of living room. Just the three of them, but Alex could tell the others were waiting outside.

Alice was being very friendly and explaining things to him, and he was glad she was friendly because he was beginning to realise that Andy would have to leave soon, and he'd be all alone in this strange place. He couldn't concentrate on what she was saying but got the general gist. She wanted to know if he had any questions and he couldn't think of any; he felt stupid. Andy gave her some details and she filled in a couple of forms; she said she'd show him his room, and they all went out to the car to bring in Alex's things. What seemed like a dozen mixed youngsters were out there, ears pricked for info, desperate to find out who the new boy was. Alex felt their eyes on him like vultures. They must all have been at least two years older than him. One, the scariest, was dressed in black with chains on his trousers and a tuft of scarlet in his black hair. Several wore baseball caps. There were a couple of girls with identical long hair, tight jeans and pierced belly buttons. None of them smiled; they looked pretty hostile. That was all the detail Alex got as he followed Andy and Alice out to the car for his stuff, and it was enough to scare him.

Alice said she would take them straight up to Alex's room; and as they walked through the crowd, a spiteful voice sounded: 'Bin bags!' Alice turned and said, 'Scipio, I'll deal with you later,' and led the way up the stairs, sniggers ringing in Alex's burning ears. This wouldn't do, he thought, he couldn't stay here, he'd have to run away.

His room was okay, and he didn't have to share with anyone. There was a bed, a wardrobe, a chest of drawers, a mirror, curtains; all in shades of pastel blue. Clean and warm enough but not exactly welcoming. There was a lock on the door.

After they had put his things away, Alice offered them some supper and Andy said he'd get away back up the road straight after that. They went back downstairs, and Alice left them in her office while she fetched a tray of tea and toast. 'Okay? What do you think so far?' asked Andy.

'Great,' lied Alex.

'You reckon you'll be all right then?'

'Fine.'

'It's only for a while till I get foster carers organised.'

'Or till my Mum's out of hospital.'

'Yeah.'

And all too soon there he was, standing in the driveway with Alice's hand on his shoulder, waving Andy off into the dark night.

'You'll be all right here, Alex,' Alice murmured, 'I'll introduce you to the others and that'll satisfy their curiosity for tonight. They're not as scary as they look.'

So they went back indoors. The circle had re-formed. 'Everybody,' she said, 'this is Alex. He'll only be here for a few days and I want you all to be nice to him. Alex is only ten; there aren't any foster carers available.'

'Who's to buddy him?' asked one of the baseball cap wearers. Alex wondered what that meant.

'Me,' said the boy in black with the scarlet flash in his hair. 'Alice said.'

'Alex, this is Malkie. He'll be your buddy for the next day or two, he'll show you round and tell you anything you need to know. Okay?'

Alex nodded. Malkie was the scariest looking of them all, but he was hardly in a position to pick and choose.

'Right then Alex,' said Alice, 'Here's your name plate. Put it up on your door; everybody has to knock before coming in. And here's your key.' Everyone was clustering round again, craning to look at the cardboard plate which bore Alex's name. The voice which had uttered 'bin bags' in such distaste earlier on broke forth again. 'Alex Bean!' Alex was used to being teased about Mr. Bean and prepared himself for the usual jokes. But the voice went on: 'Alexander Bean. Is that your name?'

'Yes,' whispered Alex, trying to sound assertive.

'Alexander Bean! Sawney Bean! You're a cannibal!' And everyone stepped back three paces.

'Scipio!' said Alice, 'I'm warning you...'

'Better watch out everybody! Don't let him get too close! He'll eat you!'

Cannibal? Alex hadn't a clue what Scipio was on

about. 'But I'm a vegetarian,' he lied, the first thing that popped into his head.

'Aye that'll be right!' said Scipio, before being warned back by Alice.

'Come on,' said Malkie, 'I'll take you upstairs.' And the two of them trudged up the stairs, Alex's stomach in knots. They came to the room door and Malkie showed him how to hang his name card up. 'Is your name really Sawney Bean?' said Malkie.

'No, it's Alex Bean. Who's Sawney Bean?'

'A cannibal. Just ignore Scipio, he's a bully, he'll leave you alone if you don't let him see that he's getting to you. I'll knock your door in the morning and take you down to breakfast.'

'What time?'

'A bell rings. About eight o'clock. See you then.' And Malkie turned on his heel and went off, the chains on his trousers jangling as he plodded back up the corridor. Alex let himself into his room, locked the door behind him, and slid down onto the floor with his back to the door, his arms around his knees and his head down. He felt the tears begin, and decided not to stop them. He sobbed.

CHAPTER THREE

Alice told Alex she'd wait a couple of days before registering him at the local school, as he'd probably be moving on. And for the first day at any rate, there were things to be done; he had to see the local doctor. And he didn't have any clothes, so Alice was taking him into Girvan, the nearest town, for some emergency supplies.

One way and another, his first day in care passed quite quickly and without any disasters. The older kids were all at school so it was quiet. Alice seemed nice, and suggested he phone and let his mother know where she was, and how she could contact him. He did so; she wasn't well enough to take the call but he left a message with the

Charge Nurse.

By the time he and Alice came back from Girvan with his new clothes, there was still half hour before the others were due home. Alice was busy so he explored the house. Seaview looked as if once, long ago, it had been quite a grand family home. It had huge tall bay windows at the front, big high ceilings, big rooms. But then there were little tight corridors that ran here and there, and Alex realised that there were different extensions which had smaller, more modern rooms; and the little corridors connected the old building with the various new bits. It was confusing, but he walked round it a few times and reckoned he could remember it.

All the bedrooms were on the first floor, in one of the extensions. There was a name plate on each door and he stared at these in turn, trying to get some clues about his fellow residents. For a start, he couldn't find a room with the name Scipio on it. Either Scipio lived in a different wing, or Scipio wasn't his real name. There wasn't a Malkie either; but there was a 'Malcolm Butler', and he thought that Malkie could be short for Malcolm. There were another four boys' names on the doors, and three girls' names. That made ten in total. Only ten? Last night it had felt like a hundred.

He heard the door opening downstairs and voices; the others were back. Quickly he locked himself into his room, and stayed there till someone knocked and shouted. It was Malkie, come to collect him for tea. So he went downstairs again, not much less scared than last night.

It started the minute he walked in the door. 'Hey Sawney,' called Scipio, 'ripped out anybody's liver and kidneys recently?' Everybody sniggered.

'Hope his teeth arenae too sharp,' joined in someone else.

'Watch an no sit too close,' started another, but fell silent as Alice came in.

Tea was okay – for the meat-eaters at any rate. Lasagne, chips and salad. Alex of course was pretending to be a vegetarian to try and stave off the cannibal accusations so he had macaroni cheese, chips and salad. It was all right. Scipio informed the whole table that he was glad he for one wasn't fat because he'd be much less interesting for a cannibal to eat. 'You'd better watch out though, Birnie,' he said to another boy who was a little on the chubby side. Birnie blushed and choked on his chips. 'Shut up Scipio,' said Malkie, and everyone watched to see what would happen next.

'Who are you tellin to shut up?' glared Scipio, but Malkie ignored him and Scipio said nothing else, but just ate his tea silently. Alex wished he was as brave as Malkie.

'Who's on dishes?' asked one of the girls and Alex realised there was a rota, and his name hadn't been put on it yet.

'That's no fair,' started someone, and again Malkie intervened – 'he's only just in the door, give him a chance.' Alex realised there was some hope for him after all; Malkie, the black-clad be-chained one, who looked more evil than all the others put together, looked like he might save him from the mob.

Next morning, Alex asked Sarah to tell him about Sawney Bean, but she didn't know much about him as she wasn't local. 'All I know is he lived in a cave up the coast round here somewhere, centuries ago. I think he had a big family. That's all I heard.'

A cleaner was mopping the kitchen floor; 'Hello,' she said, 'you're new. My name's Rita. What's yours?'

'Alex.'

'Hi Alex.'

'Rita, do you know anything about Sawney Bean?'

'He was a cannibal,' she said. 'He ate people.'

'Don't you know anything else about him?'

'There's a book about him in the post office. Along the main street.'

So Alex set off to the village to look for the post office. The post office turned out to be a sweetie shop as well, with giant jars of things you had to have weighed. Soor plooms. Dolly Mixtures. Cinammon Balls. Alex peered about among the magazines and found a little shelf with books on it. There was a small booklet with a peach-coloured cover and the title 'On The Trail Of SAWNEY BEAN And His CANNIBAL FAMILY', by somebody called Ron Deen. The book was £1.99 and Alex didn't have £1.99, so he decided to read the book in the shop, for a few minutes anyway.

His heart beat fast as he perused the story which was giving him so much trouble. It all took place more than four hundred years ago. Sawney had a huge family and they lived in the cliffs around Ballantrae and ambushed lone travellers as they made their way down the deserted coastline. Alex shivered, remembering how lonely it had been the other night for him and Andy, even though they had been safe in the old blue Escort. He came to a particularly gory bit in the story – '...cannibals cut her throat, sucking the flowing blood as wine, after which they disembowelled the victim...'

'Can I help you son?' asked a voice from above. It

was the sweetie shop owner, leaning over the newspaper counter.

Alex quickly stuffed the book back on the shelf. 'Forty pence worth of jelly babies and a ten-pence mix-up please,' he said, fishing coins out of his pocket.

Alice met him as he was coming back into Seaview. 'Alex, Andy phoned. Want to come into the office for a minute?'

Alex's heart leapt. Maybe he was moving on, maybe even tonight! Would it be to foster carers or back to his mum's? 'Am I going away?' he asked.

'Not yet, I'm afraid. He says he spent all of today trying to locate new carers for you, nearer home, but for all sorts of reasons, no-one's available.'

Alex's face fell. 'What about my mum?'

'He's been to see her and says to tell you she sends you her love but she's not feeling very well. He wants us to organise to take you up to Glasgow to visit her in hospital, and we'll do that if we can get staff cover organised.'

'When?'

'Well it'd need to be a weekend, and this weekend is out because we don't have the staff, but it could maybe be the following Saturday – I'll look into it.'

'A week on Saturday.'

'Yes. Maybe.'

'Can't I go sooner?'

'We don't have enough staff.'

'I don't need staff to visit my Mum. I could go alone.'

'Too far; you might get lost; it wouldn't be allowed.'

Alex said nothing. All of a sudden he really wanted to see his Mum, more than anything else. How could he get to Glasgow, he wondered? Alice cut in on his thoughts: 'Hot chocolate?' He nodded, and they went through to the kitchen together, while Alice asked him about his day. Alex answered absently; a plan was forming in his mind. He'd find out how to get to Glasgow, and visit his Mum, straight after the others went to school tomorrow. It would be so good to see her. If there wasn't a bus there might be a train. Or he could wave down a lorry and ask for a lift. There were plenty lorries going up and down the road outside Seaview. At teatime he quietly asked Malkie, 'Those lorries going up and down. Where do they go?'

'Stranraer. Ferry to Belfast.'

'Belfast? In Ireland?'

'Northern Ireland. Yes. It's only about an hour from Stranraer to Belfast.'

'How far away is Stranraer?'

'About half an hour in a car. That's where the lorries go when they come off the ferry. Most of them anyway I think. Stranraer to Glasgow. Why do you want to know?'

But Malkie had given Alex the information he needed. 'Oh nothing,' he replied, and finished his veggieburger. He had some thinking to do.

CHAPTER FOUR

The next morning was to be Alex's last day of freedom; Alice said he'd have to be registered at school the following week. He walked back to the main street to look out for lorries heading past for Glasgow. There was a reasonably steady stream of them; it would just be a question of getting one of them to stop. He stood right out at the edge of the kerb and waved to each of them as they went past, but they just thundered on. After a while he decided to head for the sweetie shop; he'd gone off the idea of hitching a ride to Glasgow. That book was in the same place on the shelf, so he opened it again and read another few paragraphs. '… cannibals were brought at length to justice, having subsisted for many years on the bodies of children…' He was grossed out. No wonder Scipio and that lot didn't want him near them. How could people eat other people?

'Do you want to buy that book?' said the voice from above – the shopkeeper again – and Alex quickly put it down, and bought a Cadbury's Flake. The shopkeeper said, 'the cave's pretty difficult to get to nowadays.'

'What cave?'

'Sawney Bean's cave.'

'You mean there's an actual cave you can go to? His cave?'

'Well like I say, it's difficult to get to. The Council doesn't like people nosing about because it's so dangerous and they're fed up rescuing people who fall and get hurt. Twenty-five pence please.'

'Where is it?' asked Alex, handing over the money.

'About a mile up the coast,' said the shopkeeper, gesturing. 'Don't go there though. It's way too dangerous. Next please...'

Alex left the shop and walked up to the end of the village heading north, the direction of the cave according to the shopkeeper. Should he just go right now? If there was a real cave there, then the story must be true and he might as well kill himself. But maybe it wasn't true. He wouldn't know unless he checked it out.

The tide was out but it was cold and windy, with rain threatening. He started off down the beach, but the iciness of the wind took his breath away. He decided to go back to Seaview for his jacket. By then though, the older kids were coming home from school, and he didn't want to be followed. And then it was tea-time – egg, beans and chips, but no sausages – sausages were for the kids who didn't have the shame of cannibals in their family history. Then everyone was watching Malcolm in the Middle on the telly, and he couldn't get a chance to get away after that without being seen. Then it was dark and he'd missed his chance.

However at bedtime he looked out of his bedroom window and saw that the wind had dropped and there was a beautiful full moon, filling the whole night with a silvery glow, and decided that maybe he hadn't missed his chance after all. Carefully and quietly he eased open his bedroom window and leaned out. There was a fire escape right outside his window and it was a matter of moments to step right out there. He paused and listened; no sounds from the house. He decided he would just go on a reccae expedition along the beach a bit, try to find the rough location of the cave, and go back the next day in daylight.

He reached back into the room for his jacket then padded quietly down the fire escape and out into the silver night.

CHAPTER FIVE

Alex had a little torch in his pocket, but the moon was so high and bright, and reflected so vividly in the sea, that he didn't need it. In fact it was so bright that he had to keep himself under cover; he took the first opening down towards the beach that he came to, to get away from the gaze of passers-by.

As he left the village behind and struck out round the coastline, under the cliffs, he was struck by the loneliness of the area. According to the book in the sweetie shop, the big Bean family used to catch lone travellers and drag them back to their cave. It was certainly very lonely round here; it would probably be a long time before a lone traveller was missed. Alex shivered. He hoped there weren't any cannibals in the caves now. It would be breakfast time before he was missed at Seaview – quite long enough for a cannibal to have him killed and roasted on a spit.

The moon lit up the cliff face beautifully, and revealed every crack and fissure. There were several openings that looked as if they might be caves. In each of these, Alex leaned in with his torch at the full length of his arm and shone it around; they were all just little alcoves, not proper caves at all. And then he found one whose opening was narrower than most, but which seemed to go back a bit further. He ducked down under a low ledge and crawled on his hands and knees inside. It was completely black; he picked up a pebble and threw it into the darkness ahead of him, and it appeared to go a long distance before landing with a little plop. There must be water in the cave. He switched his torch on; the little beam swept up and around, revealing a narrow passage which seemed to give way to an opening up ahead. He crawled forward, turned a corner, and sure enough, here was a big wide cavern, bigger than his bedroom at Seaview but an awkward shape. You couldn't have put a single bed up because the ground wasn't level enough. But you could probably fit about twenty cannibals in. He reached out a hand to steady himself and recoiled in horror as his hand came up against something slimy. 'Only seaweed, ya numpty,' he told himself, 'calm down.'

Alex peered around the cave and imagined the Bean family sitting around in here four centuries ago, a fire burning in the middle, its smoke curling up through the cracks in the roof. A big black cauldron bubbling over the fire, with an unmentionable stew simmering gently. Hungry cannibals perched all round the ledges gnawing at huge bones; slevers running down their chins; the children being thrown the fingers and toes. Help! Sweating and terrified, and turned to go.

He rushed too fast and hit his head on an overhanging rock; he fell over and splashed into a puddle. Imagining a bony hand reaching out from behind him to drag him back, he rushed on, slithering and splashing through puddles which hadn't been there on his way in. The tide was coming in. He stumbled through the outer crevice and back into the blinding moonlight. His heart was hammering but he couldn't stop. The sea was lapping at the foot of the cliffs and his feet were soaked through his trainers in no time. He had no idea how far he had walked along the cliff before finding the cave; it had taken a long time because he'd searched in every crevice. But he couldn't afford to take so long going back, because the sea was racing in now. Already he was wet up to his thighs, as the bigger waves crashed in.

The sea raced towards him. It was icy in the water; for the first time he understood hypothermia. If he fell in there and got swept away, it wouldn't matter how strong a swimmer he was. The temperature would kill him. He looked up the cliffside; there wasn't a path but there were plenty places where you could get a hand or foothold; some low bushes which would help him scramble up. With such a good moon he should be okay. So up he went. It wasn't easy and he slithered down several times before reaching a spot where he could rest and plan his next move. He sat there gasping, clinging to a small gorse bush that clung to the side of the hill.

Four hundred years ago, he thought, this must have been a terrifying place. That cave could easily have housed a huge cannibal family. The thought both scared and depressed him. It was all true. There was no point in denying it. That must be why his grandfather used to say 'Stay away fae Ballantrae'. It was as good as an admission of guilt. He was descended from cannibals. Tears filled his eyes and he sat there clinging to the gorse bush till he realised he was freezing. Rising stiffly to his feet, he found a path up to the road, then into the village, and within another half hour he was back at Seaview.

He climbed up the fire escape and in his bedroom window without any further difficulties, and collapsed on the floor. He had to go to the loo before going to bed, so he quietly unlocked the door and tiptoes down the corridor; and as he walked into the toilets, came face to face with Malkie, in black pyjamas.

Both boys jumped out of their skin; neither had expected to find anyone out and about. Malkie looked at Alex and whispered: 'You're still dressed!'

'Just going to the toilet.'

'You got dressed just to go to the toilet?'

'Yeah, well, let me just...' Alex made as if to pass on his way, but Malkie put out his arm and wouldn't let him by.

'You're soaked. You've been out. I can smell the sea off you. There's blood on your head. You've been on the beach!'

Alex didn't try to deny it. 'Don't tell anyone.'

'I won't, if you tell me what you were doing.'

Alex looked at the older boy. He wouldn't have expected Malkie to be interested in what anyone else was doing. But then Malkie always looked so unhappy, it was difficult to figure out what might interest him. He decided to tell Malkie everything. 'Come back to my room,' he whispered.

'Okay.'

CHAPTER SIX

Malkie fetched the downie from his own room, and the two boys sat wrapped up in their downies on the floor, with the light off so as not to attract attention, and the curtains open to let the moonlight flood in. Alex had changed out of his wet clothes and was beginning to warm up. He found the Flake he'd bought earlier on and halved it with Malkie. 'Thanks,' said Malkie, 'bet it was cold out there.'

'Freezing,' nodded Alex.

'So what were you up to?'

Where to begin? Alex searched around in his head for a way to make it sound quite normal to go exploring a treacherous coastline in the middle of the night. But he couldn't find the right words. 'I had to find Sawney Bean's cave,' he eventually said, his head sunk low into his shoulders. 'I had to find out if it was true. And it is.'

'What's true?' asked Malkie.

'The cave's there. You can see where they all sat round the campfire. You can tell it was a lonely spot and nobody would have missed travellers for ages because it's so isolated. So Sawney and his family must have just nobbled people as they passed by.'

'It's just a legend,' said Malkie.

Alex looked at him: 'What do you mean, just a legend?'

'It's not true.'

'Yes it is. There's a book.'

'Not everything you read in books is true.'

'Isn't it?'

'Of course it isn't. Did you ever see a book about Little Red Riding Hood?'

'Yes but that's different.'

'How is it different?'

'Little Red Riding Hood's just a story.'

'So is Sawney Bean.'

Alex stared at him. It was all right for him to dismiss Sawney Bean as a legend, he didn't have to share a name with him. 'I wish you were right.'

'I'll prove it to you.'

'How?'

'Research,' said Malkie, and began to explain...

The next morning, being Saturday, Alex was introduced to Circle Time as he'd never known it before. All the staff and young people in Seaview met in the lounge. Chairs had been put out in a big circle, so everybody could

30

see everybody else. It was quite scary. A member of staff called Colin, whom Alex hadn't met before because Colin had been on Days Off, chaired the meeting.

'Okay,' said Colin, 'let's get started and then we'll get finished sharpish. First off – welcome to Alex.' And he started clapping, for everyone else to join in – which they did. Alex was mortified. 'Everything okay with you, Alex?' said Colin. Alex nodded and Colin moved on. 'Next: the painters will be in next week doing the hallway up, so we're going to use the back door till it's finished, and rope off the wet bits. Any questions? Good. Next: there's a disco on in the village hall tonight, over-14s only. If you want to go, give me your name at the end. It's £2 to get in. Next: if anybody knows anything about the broken pool cue I'd like them to tell me about it. Until I find out what's happened, pool is off. Well?'

A circle of faces gazed at him, startled. Alex felt guilty for no reason, and looked at Scipio, who he knew had broken the cue by using it as a pole vault. Scipio was staring at Birnie, nodding at him, making him speak up. Birnie was nervous and gulped a bit, and said 'aw Colin that's no fair.'

'What's not fair, Brendan?' Colin was calm, and ready to listen.

'I mean it wasnae naebody here, it must have been a mistake, it was broken anyway…'

'Anybody agree, or disagree, with Brendan?' asked Colin, looking round the room, holding everyone's gaze in turn with solemn eyes. Utter silence. 'Well,' said Colin, 'it was certainly an old pool cue but it was perfectly useable. People who want to play pool have to respect the equipment, you all know that.'

Malkie spoke up; Alex couldn't believe how calm he was. 'If we find out who broke it, will the cue be replaced?'

'That depends,' said Colin, 'on whether the person or persons who broke the original is willing to buy a new one.'

There was a gasp. Malkie paused, then continued: 'But that was an old cue, and new ones are expensive. Everyone would get the benefit of a new cue. How would it be if half the cost of the new cue were provided by anyone who knew anything about breaking the old one?'

'Half?' said Colin, 'do you know how much these things cost?'

'Too much for anybody to be able to replace it straight away,' said Malkie, 'this way, we can probably get the pool table up and running again by teatime... don't you think?' he added, looking straight at Scipio. Scipio's eyes narrowed and he gave a short nod.

Colin accepted this suggestion. 'Speak to me before lunchtime then,' he said. 'Okay. Newsround. What's been happening?' and he went round everybody in turn and made them say what had been happening that week. Everybody else had to listen. It was fascinating. In ten minutes, Alex got to hear about maths homework, football practice, forthcoming reviews and children's hearings, appointments at the orthodontist, trouble on the high school bus, the school play. When it came his turn he managed to squeak 'I'm fine.'

At the end of the meeting everyone seemed relaxed and businesslike. The staff left the youngsters alone and Malkie spoke across the room directly to Scipio. 'Got a tenner, Scipio?'

'I was saving it for my sister's birthday.'

'You should have been more careful with the pool cue then.'

'Get him to accept seven fifty.'

'I already beat him down from twenty. It'll have to be ten.'

Scipio paused. The others all looked at him sideways, except for Malkie whose eyes were fearless. 'It wasn't just me that broke it,' began Scipio.

'Yes it was. And if you don't stump up, there'll be no more pool. Nobody else helped you pole vault off the sofa.' Alex held his breath. How come Malkie was so brave? Scipio looked round carelessly. 'Keep your hair on. S'only a tenner. Here. Take it.' And he tossed a crumpled brown note at Malkie and strolled nonchalantly out of the room.

Later that afternoon Sarah drove the minibus to Girvan with Colin, Alex, Charlene, Malkie and Birnie, and they went to the swimming pool. Afterwards in the café, Alex got a few moments alone with Malkie, and asked him how he managed to handle Scipio. Malkie was stirring his hot chocolate and looked up as he replied: 'I'm not afraid of him. And he knows that. That's how I handle him. He only bullies people who let themselves be bullied. I'm better than him, and so are most people. So why should we be afraid of him? It's just a question of believing in yourself.'

Just a question of believing in yourself. Alex pondered that one. Did he believe in himself? Only some of the time. But that old cannibal had got in the way of his self-belief recently. 'Do you believe in yourself?' he asked Malkie.

Malkie didn't smile: 'I might be scum but I'm clever scum. That's what I believe about myself. Anyway, listen,' he said, 'we'll start the research while we get the chance. Colin and Sarah will give us an hour in the shops before we go back to the ranch. There's free Internet in the library. We'll go there.' Mystified, Alex agreed, and thanked his lucky stars he had fallen in with the right scum.

CHAPTER SEVEN

The library in Girvan had a room at the back with six computers, all with Internet access. To use them, you had to be a member; Malkie of course had a ticket. The librarian greeted him by name: 'Morning Malcolm, how's things?'

'Great thanks. Can I have an hour? This is my friend, he's just sitting along with me, if that's okay.'

'No problem. Anything you need any help with, just ask. Take number three,' she said, nodding to the PC in the furthest corner. 'There's room for two chairs.'

'While we're at it,' said Malkie, 'we're researching this local legend, the one about the cannibal. Sawney Bean. Do you have any books on him?'

'One or two, I'll show you.'

'Tell you what, he'll come with you,' said Malkie

nodding at Alex, 'and collect the books. And you bring them back over to the PC, okay?'

'Okay,' said Alex obediently. His esteem for Malkie was growing by the minute. Libraries were a mystery as far as he was concerned; but Malkie seemed to expect to get some answers here. He followed the librarian to a display stand where there were lots of books and old photos of Girvan and the surrounding area. And there was the book from the sweetie shop! As well as one or two other, thicker, heavier tomes which Alex knew he wouldn't be patient enough to read.

'I'll just take that one, thanks' he said, pointing.

'You'd better mention the other two to Malkie,' said the librarian, 'he likes to be thorough.'

Nearly skipping with joy, Alex dashed back to the PC section with his trophy in his hand. 'Look!' he beamed, 'the book in the sweetie shop!'

Malkie looked up, put a finger to his lips and indicated other people in the library, and pointed at the PC screen.

'At least a dozen websites,' he said. 'Some of them just flannel but some good stuff too.'

'How can you tell the difference?' murmured Alex, mystified.

'Proper sources. Balanced arguments. Facts, not opinions. More than one source of evidence. That sort of thing.' Alex looked blank, and Malkie added, 'you get it in history at school.'

Alex sat open-mouthed for a while as Malkie whizzed through websites, cutting and pasting bits of information onto a word document as he went. At least that's what he said he was doing; Alex couldn't follow and they only had an hour, so he let Malkie point and click and double-click while he turned his attention to the book.

'...Beyond, in the shadows, lay the silent watchful cannibals who, after desperate fighting and pursuit, were apprehended and conducted to the Tolbooth Jail in Edinburgh...'

'According to this,' said Malkie, looking at the screen, 'James VI brought an army of four hundred men, with bloodhounds, to try and hunt Sawney down. There should be evidence of that elsewhere.'

Alex was getting fidgety. He lost interest in the pamphlet and went off for a browse around the bookshelves. All the Harry Potters were out, but there was a full set of Lemony Snickets, so he pulled one out and had a look. 'If my mother could see me now,' he thought with amusement, 'sitting on a sunny Saturday afternoon in a library, reading a book! She'd think I'd been abducted by aliens.' But really it was very peaceful in the library, and the story was good, and his chair was a good old solid wooden one that wouldn't be easily thrown at you in a fight, and he found himself quite engrossed. Malkie came and found him when the hour on the PC was up and they walked down the library steps together. 'That was good,' said Alex, 'can we come again?'

'Any time you like,' said Malkie. 'I'm here three or four times a week. Anyway. Sawney Bean. There are loads of references to him, but I think they're a bit far-fetched. Like the story about James VI bringing an army. Surely we'd know about that from other sources? You'd think it'd be big news. I'm going to speak to my history teacher.'

As they walked back to the car park to meet the

others, they came on a wedding party. A girl in a big white frock and a bloke in a kilt were posing outside an old house, having their photos taken. 'Is that a church?' asked Alex.

'Registry Office.'

'What, births and deaths and all that?' Alex remembered going to the Registry Office in Glasgow with his mother, to register the death of his granddad.

'Yeah.'

They walked on a few more paces, then both boys had the idea at the same time. They stopped and looked at each other. 'Birth certificates,' said Malkie.

'Death certificates,' said Alex.

'Not everyone registered in those days,' said Malkie.

'But Sawney might have,' said Alex, 'don't you think?'

'Maybe.'

Colin and Sarah and Birnie and Charlene were standing at the minibus, waiting for them, just across the road. There was no time to do anything else in Girvan. 'We'll talk later,' said Malkie, and they rejoined the others and headed back to Seaview.

Alex had to go to school on Monday; the only kid from Seaview who was young enough to go to the local primary school. It was okay; as schools went. School wasn't Alex's favourite way of spending his time but the teacher seemed okay.

After school, Alex went to the post office again, and bought two crème eggs; one for him, and one for his new best friend Malkie. Malkie got history on Mondays and had said he was going to have a word with his history teacher about something called 'old parish records'. Alex watched Malkie coming in from school with the others, and gave him ten minutes to get changed; then couldn't wait any longer, and went and knocked on Malkie's door. Malkie let him in, took the egg and opened it straight away, and told Alex what Mr. Wilson had said, through a mouthful of chocolate and white and yellow goo.

'Old Parish Records,' he said, 'are how births and deaths and marriages used to be recorded, before it became a council job, sometime in the nineteenth century. It was the job of the local minister, or maybe the session clerk, of the kirk, to keep a record in a big book of everybody who was born or married or died in his parish.'

'Can we go and look?'

'It depends. Some of the records got lost, or burnt, and not everyone was recorded anyway.'

'But if Sawney Bean's was recorded, we could try and see if we could find it.'

'Yes. We could.'

'So where are the records kept?'

'Mainly in Edinburgh. There's a place called Register House, Mr. Wilson says, that has copies of all the old parish records from all over Scotland. So you can find all the births, deaths and marriages there, so long as the person you were looking for was born or died or got married in Scotland.'

'That's it then!' said Alex. 'When are we going?'

'It's not as easy as all that,' said Malkie. 'How would we get there, for one thing? Edinburgh's miles away. And we could go all that way and still not find anything.'

Alex wasn't giving up now. He was fed up being bullied; he didn't like the way all the kids except Malkie had adopted the nickname Sawney for him; and he was desperate for a big meaty beefburger. Much more macaroni cheese and he'd scream. 'We've got to go and find out if Sawney Bean was real!' he said. 'I've got to prove that I'm not related to him. Please, Malkie, I'd go myself but I wouldn't be able to find the old parish wrecks that you're talking about, I really need your help.'

They heard Sarah's voice shouting 'teatime!' up the stairs, and the thunder of hooves as the kids went charging down to get fed. 'Look,' said Malkie, 'I've been glad to help you so far, but going to Edinburgh's different.' He saw Alex's face, and added, 'if you can find a way of getting us to Edinburgh and back, safely and without getting arrested or run over by a bus or kidnapped or anything else that might happen, I'll consider it. Okay?'

'Fantastic!' said Alex joyfully.

'But I need a proper plan of action,' warned Malkie.

'I'll sort it out!' said Alex, and the two of them went downstairs for their tea. Chicken nuggets; vegetarian option, Crispy Pancakes. Alex was more determined than ever, pushing bits of unidentifiable yellow stuff round his plate, to clear his name and get back to meat-eating. He had a lot of catching up to do.

But how to get to Edinburgh. He was chewing his Crispy Pancake and pondering, when Scipio's voice broke in through the fog of his thoughts.

'You should see her car,' he was boasting. 'Massive. Two months old. Probably pays for it out of the mileage she gets for coming to visit me.... my Mum says you get a great view, it's so high up. They're all coming down in it tomorrow night for my review.'

'What is it?' asked someone else.

'Jeep Cherokee. Like an army tank. Huge. Massive wheels, cost a fortune just to buy a new tyre.'

'What time's your review at?'

'Four o'clock, straight after school but I'm dogging off the afternoon, I'll be here in time to get changed and organised. My mum and dad'll probably get here with my social worker about half three. Depends on the traffic leaving Edinburgh, my social worker says. Takes about two hours to get here.'

Alex's ears pricked up. A big car, big boot probably. Coming from Edinburgh and no doubt returning there too. Two hours' journey. That was it! He was afraid to catch Malkie's eye in case his excitement was spotted and he gave the game away; but when he sneaked a look, Malkie was plodding his way through his chicken nuggets, completely wrapped up in his own thoughts. He must not have heard Scipo talking, or more likely he had just ignored him. Alex's mind raced. This was it. All systems go. And he began to lay his plans.

CHAPTER EIGHT

Malkie wasn't keen. We'll get caught before we're out of Ballantrae,' he said. Alex couldn't believe his ears. A heaven-sent opportunity like this, and Malkie was just going to let it pass by?

'We won't get caught,' he argued.

'We'll suffocate in the boot.'

'It's a huge car.'

'Have you ever been locked up in a tiny space for two hours at a time?'

'No, but...'

'Well I have. It's horrible. And I'm not doing it again, right?' Malkie's voice was rising as he spoke – it wasn't like him to lose his cool – and Alex recognised a note of panic. He'd never asked why Malkie lived in a children's home, instead of at home with his parents – it was too intrusive. But he began to wonder.

The pair were silent for a while. They were outside behind the house, at the basketball hoop, bouncing a ball about so as to look normal. Birnie drifted along and joined them, and they threw some hoops for a while; then it began to get dark so they went inside. There was no more chance to talk till bedtime. Alex's bedtime was half an hour earlier than the others, so he waited in his room until all the sounds in the corridor had subsided, then slipped along and knocked on Malkie's door. Malkie seemed to be expecting him: 'Look Alex, I'm sorry but I can't do it. There'll be another chance. We could just get on a bus, for goodness' sake.'

'That's okay Malkie,' said Alex, 'but I'm going to have a go. I just want you to tell me what to do when I get there.'

'You're going alone?' Malkie was astonished. 'Are you sure?'

'Dead sure,' said Alex. He was far from confident that he'd be able to find Register House, never mind check the records. But he was so desperate for action, he couldn't *not* take this chance.

Malkie said nothing for a while. Then he got out a piece of paper and a pencil. 'Take your mobile and make use it's charged up. Have you got money in it? What you should probably do is talk to somebody at the desk and ask them to help you...'

'Thanks Malkie – I'll text you.'

'Better go to bed now,' said Malkie, 'I'll write you a list for tomorrow tea-time.'

Next day at school, Alex was nervous and twitchy. He couldn't wait for his adventure to begin, and was terrified he'd let something slip that would let the cat out of the bag. At three o'clock he rushed straight home – what if Scipio's review was brought forward, and the social worker left early, and he missed his chance?

He was just entering the gate at Seaview when a huge truck-shaped car drove in past him. His heart hammered in excitement. His freedom chariot! Scipio must have been waiting just inside – he came rushing out, his face all lit up – then the car scrunched to a halt on the gravel and a young woman jumped out. She was alone.

'Where are they?' screamed Scipio. 'Why didn't you bring my mum and dad? They said they were coming, why didn't you bring them?' His face was scarlet and Alex, caught in a position where he had no choice but to watch, realised Scipio was nearly crying.

'I'm sorry Godfrey,' said the social worker, putting an arm out to him' ('Godfrey!!' thought Alex). 'I went to collect them at one o'clock as planned, but they weren't there. There was no-one in. I tried round at your Aunt Selma's house, but she said she hadn't seen them. I went back and waited fifteen minutes, but there was no sign of them. I had to come away or I'd have been late.'

'This is so typical,' sobbed Scipio, and gave a massive kick at the wheel of the car, just as Alice came out to join them. She took the scene in, raised an eyebrow at the social worker, and held the door open to let Alex through. He escaped upstairs; the last thing he heard were Scipio's furious words, 'that's their last chance, I'm never going back...'

Alex was shocked. He was beginning to see that there were all sorts of reasons for kids living here, most of them pretty unpleasant. He actually felt sorry for Scipio (Godfrey?!) in a way which surprised him.

45

Meantime however – what would this mean for his plan? Would the review go ahead without Scipio's parents? When would the social worker be heading back to Edinburgh?

Alex emptied his school bag of books and jotters, and filled it with stuff for a journey – a hoody sweatshirt, a woolly hat, a can of Irn Bru, a tube of Smarties, his torch, his Walkman and a couple of CDs. He changed into his jeans and trainers and a long-sleeved tee-shirt, then slipped downstairs with his bag and stashed it in a cupboard under the stairs where he'd be able to grab it quickly on the way out. Then he went to the kitchen and got a drink of milk and a chocolate chip cookie, and waited for Malkie to come home.

The mood around the tables was subdued at teatime. The Cherokee was still in the driveway but Scipio's review was over. He and his social worker were through in the office, talking with Alice. Everybody felt the shame of one's parents not turning up at something as important as a review, and the conversation was muttered.

'Didn't turn up last time either,' whispered one.

'If that was me I'd go raj,' whispered another.

Alex and Malkie had worked out their plan of action. After tea they went outside, Alex picking his bag up en route. They walked right outside the gate, as if going for a walk, then squatted down behind the wall where nobody would see them from the house. It was beginning to get dark, and the moon was hidden behind thick clouds. The idea was that when the social worker came out to leave, and clicked the remote control to unlock the doors, Malkie would go and divert her attention while Alex jumped into the boot. Then she would get in and drive away, unknowingly taking Alex with her.

Both boys were nervous. 'How much money have you got?' asked Malkie.

Alex searched his pockets. 'Three pounds forty-seven.' Malkie gave him another two pounds eighteen. They waited on in silence, their joints stiffening as they crouched in the ditch.

At last they heard the social worker opening the front door, taking her leave. She came out onto the gravel path, pointed the remote, and the car locks all clicked open. Alex nudged Malkie who sprang into action, striding forward to speak – but she'd gone back inside, leaving the car open. 'Quick!' squeaked Alex, and threw open the back door. He gaped. No boot – just a big open space behind the back seat, and a couple of tartan rugs. Malkie looked both ways while helping Alex in, and was just about to close the door on his friend when he hesitated – looked both ways again – and at the last minute, jumped in beside Alex and quickly pulled the door shut behind him – just as they heard the social worker's voice coming back out of the house, with Scipio.

Alex and Malkie burrowed under the blankets, hearts thudding. How would they explain this if they were caught? The social worker opened the driver's door; she was still talking to Scipio, saying goodbye. Finally, she got in the car and started the engine, and they were nosing out of the main gate and off up the coast road. No-one had seen them escape. No police car with blue flashing lights and siren came racing up behind them. The radio was tuned to some screeching opera music; the social worker hummed along; and Malkie and Alex sat tight and silent as the miles sped by. So far, so good.

CHAPTER NINE

It wasn't exactly comfortable, sitting in the tailgate of the Cherokee all that way; but it wasn't exactly uncomfortable either. Thanks to the high headrests on the seats in front, Malkie and Alex were able to sit upright, side by side, facing rearwards, their knees up to their chins. It was a smooth ride and they even dozed off occasionally. After an hour and three-quarters of mainly darkness around them, street lights sprang up and they realised they were in a town, or possibly even a city. Possibly even Edinburgh itself. They listened as the social worker made a call on her hands-free:

'Hi Dave - nearly home. You okay?... no.. pig of a day.. Fancy phoning for a carry-out? Okay just coming up to Maybury... fifteen minutes, starving, could you order me lemon chicken and egg fried rice please? No spring roll. Cheers Dave.'

The boys tensed. Fifteen minutes. This was a danger

spot for them, a time when their presence might be uncovered. They squatted low again, under the rugs. The car began to stop and start, passing through traffic lights, queuing in traffic. Soon it was pulling off the main road, along a quieter street, nosing along, slowing; and reversing into a parking space. The engine was switched off. The boys held their breath. There was a short pause – the gathering of a jacket and handbag – and then the social worker was out and away, having locked the doors from outside. The car was all theirs and they hissed in excitement and relief.

'We're here! We're here!' squeaked Alex, 'we made it! Let's go!'

'Watch out, she might come back... shhh! somebody's coming!' A motorbike was pulling up alongside and they squatted down low again, listening. A doorbell rang, ten seconds passed, then 'Delivery for Paterson – twelve fifty – cheers Mate,' – and then steps and motor bike in reverse. Lemon chicken and fried rice arriving. Alex and Malkie were suddenly hungry.

'What next then?' asked Alex, deferring to his leader. Alex was concentrating.

'Okay, we need somewhere to sleep for the night. The registry place will be shut.'

'What about here, in the car? We could put the back seats down. She probably won't be back out till morning.'

'Good thinking. Yes that'll do; as soon as it gets light we'll need to get out and away in case somebody sees us.'

'I'm hungry. And stiff. Can we get out for a stretch? Go and get some chips or something?'

'We should take turns. New car like this, it'll

probably lock itself if we leave it open. You go first. Don't be away for more than fifteen minutes. Find a toilet and a chippie; get a bit of a walk; then come straight back. Eat your chips before you get back in the car, we don't want to leave a smell.'

So that's what they did. The street was very quiet, and none of the good citizens of Marchmont noticed two young boys setting out their camp for the night in the back of a Jeep Cherokee. Long before the lights had gone out in the tenement flats all round them, Alex and Malkie were fast asleep.

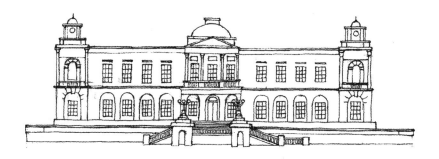

CHAPTER TEN

Next morning they were hungry again. They reasoned that taking bottles of milk from the social worker's doorstep wasn't really stealing, it was more like borrowing, because they could pay her back the next time she was down at Seaview. So they took a bottle each, while it was still dark, and drank it as they wandered along the road.

They came to a park and walked across it; not many people were about, just a few early-morning cyclists and some young kids about their own age, delivering papers. Neither of the boys had ever been to Edinburgh before. It was a fine crisp autumn morning and they enjoyed being out and about early. They came to a huge bridge and when they peered over its edge, could see way down below into what looked like another town, an old-fashioned one, deep below the surface of the one they were on. Then when they looked away to the left they could see a big castle, which they presumed must be Edinburgh Castle. Alex was excited to see, in real life, something he'd only heard about in stories before. 'That's why I want to see the records,' he explained to Malkie. 'If things really happened, you could find them, couldn't you?'

'Not always,' said Malkie. 'Sometimes things get destroyed. Like buildings. Edinburgh Castle's still there because it's so huge, but there are loads of buildings which really did exist hundreds of years ago, but got knocked down and you can't even find their site because something else has been built in its place.'

'But the records,' said Alex. 'If Sawney Bean really existed, there'd be records to prove it, wouldn't there?'

'Well I reckon there would be some kinds of records. Like, that bit about King James getting an army together to come and find him. You'd expect to find that written up somewhere. To be honest, I don't know if the births, deaths and marriages records will show us anything.'

Alex and Malkie plodded on. Alex's head was whirling. How could he prove that he wasn't anything to do with cannibals?

'Of course what you could do,' said Malkie, 'much more easily, is check back your own family tree. See what direction it takes you. You'd get all that in Register House.'

'Fantastic! We'll do that then,' said Alex.

The streets were much busier now. They passed by a huge railway station and then came out onto a long, busy shopping street. 'It's near here,' said Malkie, and soon they found it, sitting back off the main road, near a huge statue of a horse. It was a big stone building with wide steps in front, and big wooden doors – which were closed. The boys peered at the brass plaque to the left of the door. 'Open Monday to Friday, 9-4.30pm' – and it wasn't nine o'clock yet, so that was all right. The doors would soon swing open and they'd be able to get in there and find out what they needed to know.

They wandered back out onto the main street and found a clock – eight-thirty. Only half an hour to go. They debated whether to spend their dwindling resources on an Egg McMuffin to share, and decided not to. A newspaper vendor had just opened his kiosk, and as Alex and Malkie were turning back towards Register House, the vendor started bawling out his wares: 'Get yer Record here! Blair in new White House Row! Petrol Shortage! Two boys missing from care home!'

At that last announcement, Malkie and Alex froze. Two boys missing from care home? Surely that couldn't be them? Surely it was too soon for Alice and Colin to have reported them to the papers? They wanted to go back and have a closer look at the newspaper, but didn't want to arouse suspicions. Malkie told Alex to wait at Register House while he went back on his own – no-one would be looking for a single boy. But he came back to Alex within five minutes: 'Can't see anything on the front page, it must be inside. No big photos or anything, we're safe enough. Nobody will be looking for us.'

Alex didn't say anything. If a photo was put out, Malkie would be instantly recognisable, with his all-black outfit, his chains, and his tuft of scarlet hair.

As they were standing there, the big wooden doors of Register House swung open and the small queue that had formed straggled in. Alex and Malkie went in behind them, following the crowd, and were surprised to be stopped by a uniformed man at a desk. 'Sorry boys, children not allowed in.'

Quick as a flash, Malkie said, 'I'm eighteen.'

The official looked at Malkie and narrowed his eyes.

'Got any identity?'

'No, but...'

'Got seventeen pounds then?'

'Seventeen pounds?'

The official nodded at the display board on his desk. 'Day pass, seventeen pounds.'

Alex and Malkie looked at each other, shocked. Seventeen pounds! 'We'll come back later, thank you,' he said coolly to the official, and they sauntered back out of the front door. Now what?

An old woman was panting her way up the steps. She was laden with bags and coats and walked with a stick. A bright red scarf fluttered out behind her, and she didn't notice as it slithered off the back of her coat onto the steps. Alex went and picked it up: 'There's yer scarf, missus.'

The old woman stopped and looked round. 'My scarf! Thank you son, I never saw it go...'

Malkie had an idea. He quickly engaged her in conversation: 'My friend and I were just waiting here. Are you going to look at the records, missus?'

'Aye...'

'We were wanting to go in, but we didn't realise it was so expensive.'

'Aye it's no cheap but I have a season ticket.'

'A season ticket?'

'I'm here every day. I look up people's ancestors for them. Americans mostly. People who want to find out about their past.'

'That's what we want,' said Alex, and the old woman looked at him. Malkie took over:

'We're trying to find out if my friend here is descended from someone who lived about 1600.'

'That's what they all want,' said the old woman, 'they all want to be descended from Robert the Bruce or William Wallace, so they pay me good money to find out for them.'

'Is it hard to find out?' asked Malkie. 'Could I come in along with you, and could you show me how to check it out?'

'They'll no let you in, son,' said the old woman, 'you're too young. Maybe I could have a wee look for you?'

Alex gasped. 'That would be brilliant!' He loved this eccentric old woman who didn't ask awkward questions. 'But we don't have any money...'

The old woman peered at them through a thick pair of glasses. 'Well it'll make a wee change for me, and anyway you did me a good turn. And it won't take me long probably.'

They quickly gave her the details she needed, and she told them to meet her back on the steps at ten-thirty a.m., while she went off to find the information which could save Alex from a lifetime of bullying. Alex and Malkie were ecstatic, and slapped each other, high five, on the hands. Brilliant!

It was too cold just to hang about, so they went for a walk, along old back streets and into a big mall, and got back to Register House at ten-twenty-five. They waited ten minutes, getting twitchy. What if the old woman was a secret agent and had lured them here so that the police could pick them up? But no, here she was at ten-thirty-five, hirpling out to see them with her stick, clutching a notebook. Alex was nearly too nervous to stay and hear what she had to say. What if it was all true? He felt sick with excitement.

'I'm needing a cup of tea,' she said, 'there's a café round the corner.' So, with Alex's stomach churning, they all went together into a big formica-tabled café round the corner. The old woman asked them what they wanted and, mentally counting up their remaining resources and eyeing the menu, they said they'd have a small coke each. She looked at them. They looked like good kids.

'I got paid this morning, for a job I did last month. I managed to find a minor duke in the father's line of an oil widow from Texas. Let me buy this. I fancy an all-day breakfast. Want to join me? And while we're eating I'll tell you what I found out.'

Delighted, they accepted; and the old woman ordered three all-day breakfasts with an extra pot of tea and double toast. She settled down and they could see she was beginning to enjoy herself. 'Let me introduce myself,' she began. 'My name is Nettie Logie...'

CHAPTER ELEVEN

Nettie Logie may have looked eccentric, but she certainly knew her stuff. She flipped open her notebook and propped it up against the teapot so that she could read it, and butter her toast at the same time.

'I couldn't find any Sawney Beans in the sixteenth or seventeenth centuries,' she began. 'I checked under Alexander, Alex, Sandy and Zander; and also under Bean, Behan, Bevan, and any other variation of Bean I could think of. Nothing. That's not to say he didn't exist. You might not expect to find his birth certificate; not everybody registered their birth in those days. But if he was publicly executed at Edinburgh after being personally tracked down and arrested by King James VI, you'd expect there to be a record of his death.'

'So he never existed?' asked Alex, holding his breath.

'I doubt it; actually the story sounds to me like one of those propaganda tales that are made up to frighten people. You have to remember that very few ordinary people could read and write in those days; so stories were passed on by word of mouth, and would be embroidered out of all recognition in the process.

'On the other hand, you have to remember that there would be times of poor harvest or high taxes when lots of people would be starving. In those circumstances, some families might resort to cannibalism as their only source of meat. Especially lawless families who were isolated from other people.

'So my guess is that the Sawney Bean story is a myth. There may have been cannibals living in the caves along the Ayrshire coast, but I doubt if they were called Bean and I'm pretty certain they weren't brought to trial in Edinburgh... That's lovely dear,' she added as the waitress brought three massive glistening platters of bacon, sausage, eggs, black pudding, tattie scones, mushrooms, beans, and tomatoes. 'And may we have some more toast?'

Alex gazed at his bacon and sausage and black pudding longingly. This could be the end to his self-enforced vegetarianism! But he had to just double-check. 'Does that mean I'm not descended from them?'

'I was just coming to that bit. I traced your tree back, using your mother's name and date of birth as you gave them to me, and managed to get as far as 1800 before I lost the thread. The last record I found was of Thomas Graham Behan, who was an apprentice gardener at a castle somewhere in Argyll. That was his marriage record; he married at the age of eighteen.'

'But Behan's not my name.'

'It sounds close though, and remember, people couldn't read or write. So when they went to register a birth, they had to rely on the Registrar's spelling to make sure it was correct. By the time Thomas Graham Behan died, according to his death certificate, he was Head Gardener at that same castle, and his name was down as Bean. During his lifetime, it seems, the name changed from Behan to Bean.'

Malkie took up the questioning; at Nettie's last words, Alex had closed his eyes and put a whole sausage in his mouth at once, sideways, and was now blissfully chewing and swallowing and licking his lips. 'Why did the record run out in 1800?' asked Malkie.

'I suspect young Thomas may have come over from Ireland,' said Nettie. 'Behan is, I think, an Irish name, and Argyll is close to Ireland. If he was born in Ireland, his birth would be recorded there rather than here. On the other hand, it may just be that his birth wasn't recorded, or the records were destroyed through fire or whatever.'

Alex was moving on to the black pudding, his face a study of serious, concentrated contentment. Nettie spoke again: 'Records don't tell you everything but if you read between the lines you can make intelligent guesses. I think you'll find, Alex, that Sawney Bean was invented by superstitious people who wanted to warn their children against travelling alone on isolated roads. The cannibal would be a sort of bogey man. People still threaten their children with bogey men.'

'My mother used to say if I didn't behave she'd get the social worker to me,' said Malkie, and Nettie agreed enthusiastically, saying that was just the sort of thing she was talking about.

Nettie had finished her breakfast – how had she managed to hoover it up so fast, while talking all the time? – and was organising her big black bag, putting the notebook in, taking her purse out. 'Is that the time? I'd better get back to my Texan Earls. Here's my card,' she said, passing a small yellow card to Alex, 'remember me when you're rich and famous. Here's twenty pounds, could you settle the bill? Bye!' And she was off, the boys calling their thanks as she shouldered her way out of the café door.

Bliss had crept over Alex and wrapped him in its cosy embrace. 'I'm not a cannibal,' he told Malkie, grinning.

'I know you're not,' said Malkie. 'Congratulations.' They looked at Nettie's card. It read, 'Annette K.D. Logie, PhD (Edin) BA (Hons): Genealogist' and gave an address in a place called Inverleith Row.

'I'm going to send her flowers, as soon as I can afford it,' said Alex, 'she was brill.'

They finished their breakfast to the last crumb, paid the bill and left the change as a tip for the waitress, and sauntered out into the crisp Edinburgh autumn sunshine. 'What now?' said Alex, and as he spoke, they came upon the news vendor again.

'Get yer Record here! Blair in new White House Row! Petrol Shortage! Two boys missing from care home!' Alex and Malkie ducked and ran across the main road, down the railway steps, through the station and out the other side, up a big long set of steps and along a side street before they stopped, breathless. The castle was ahead of them. 'Let's go for a quick look,' said Malkie, 'before we decide what to do next.' So Alex agreed.

The castle looked very impressive, high up on its rock. But it cost £5 to get in so they couldn't see much. They wandered back down the hill and through some lanes, discussing their next move. 'I suppose we have to go back,' Malkie was saying. 'We don't have anywhere to sleep tonight in Edinburgh.'

'Do you think we're in big trouble?'

'Probably. I guess we'll be grounded for a few days.'

'It'll be worth it.'

'Yeah. But they won't be too sore on us, they'll be relieved we're safe and sound. They'll be worried about getting into trouble for letting us run away in the first place.'

'But it wasn't their fault.'

'No I know, but still...' They were walking along a terrace with big stone buildings on one side and an iron railing on the other. A poster in a café window had caught Malkie's eye: 'Goths and Alternatives Night Tonight. 7pm. All welcome.'

Alex looked at the poster and then at Malkie in his blacks and chains. 'What's an Alternative?' he asked.

'Just someone who's a bit different from other people,' said Malkie. 'Will we still be here at 7pm?'

As he spoke, a young woman came out of the café with a big folder under her arm. She saw the boys looking at the poster and spoke to them: 'thinking of coming along tonight then?'

'We might,' said Malkie, 'what sort of place is this?'

'It's a youth café.'

63

'What, just a café, for anybody?'

'Well it's a sort of youth project. You can come along if you like, the Goths and Alternatives night is an informal sort of drop-in thing. Have you got friends who come along?'

'No, I've never heard of this place before… I'm not from round here.'

'Come inside for a minute and I'll give you a leaflet. My name's Debbie, by the way,' and she held out her hand.

Malkie smiled, shook her hand and said 'Malkie… Alex,' indicating his friend.

'Hi Malkie and Alex, welcome to Edinburgh.' They were inside the café now. The only other person there was a man, definitely not a youth, sitting at a metal table reading the paper. He didn't have much hair. Debbie waved to him, 'this is Tom, my colleague. Tom, this is Malkie and Alex. Malkie might come along tonight.'

Tom smiled and raised a hand, then looked down at his paper again. Malkie was perusing a leaflet Debbie had given him; it was Alex who noticed that Tom was reading a Record, the same paper that the news vendor over at Register House had been selling.

'I don't know if we can stay around till 7pm tonight,' Malkie was saying, 'but I'll definitely come back some other time.'

'That's cool,' said Debbie.

Tom's eyes met Alex's: *'He knows,'* thought Alex.

'We're not police,' said Tom, 'but we do care about people's safety.' Alex stared at him. He didn't know what to do or say.

'So what other kind of things do you do here?' Malkie was talking to Debbie.

'Different things. We're youth workers.' ('Youth Workers?' thought Alex, 'never heard of them.') We've got projects for young people who are homeless. Or getting mixed up with drugs. Or in trouble of different kinds.'

'Oh,' said Alex, 'for example I have a friend who lives in a children's home, and will be leaving care in a couple of years' time. Would you be able to help him?'

'Yes, that's the sort of thing we're good at. Make sure you tell him about us.'

'I will... What sort of help would you give him?'

'Malkie...' interrupted Alex, nervously... 'I mean would you help him find a place to stay?'

'Yes, we would...'

'And if he wanted to go to college or uni or something, would that be okay?'

'Of course. We'd help him do whatever it was he wanted to do.'

Alex couldn't get Malkie's attention; Tom spoke to him again. 'Have you a long way to go to get home?'

'Yes,' whispered Alex.

'Need some help to get there?'

Alex nodded.

'Would you like a can of juice while we talk?'

Alex hesitated. 'Okay.'

Tom fetched three cans of Irn Bru from behind a café counter, and put the kettle on for Debbie. 'She'll have herbal tea,' he said to Alex. 'So; how did you fetch up in Victoria Terrace on a sunny day in October?' Tom smiled and sat down. Alex looked around him. The door was still open; he could run for it. But where would he run to? Malkie was looking as if he never wanted to leave this place; he wouldn't survive long without Malkie. And Tom looked trustworthy. And when it came down to it, the main thing was, *he wasn't a cannibal,* and didn't have to run away from children's homes any more to prove his innocence. He'd already done that. He sat down.

Much later, on the long drive back to Ballantrae in Andy's old blue Escort, Andy asked Malkie whether he'd enjoyed Edinburgh.

'Yeah. I made a few contacts. It was cool.'

'Thank you for looking after Alex. He needed a friend.'

They both glanced at Alex, fast asleep in the back seat. 'That's okay. I'm glad I came with him to Edinburgh – I wasn't going to at first because of being locked up, but it was good. I've got my future plans sorted out now. It was a good trip.'

'Future plans?'

'I'm going to go and live in Edinburgh and be a genealogist. And a student. And go to the Goth Group.'

'That's great,' said Andy.

'Yes, I think so too.'

CHAPTER TWELVE

Three days later it was Circle Time again at Seaview. Colin waited until everyone was seated, then began: 'Quite a bit of business to get through today, so let's get started.

'First of all, the painting is finished, and it's looking good, so thank you everybody for your co-operation.

'Next, Scipio and I have purchased the new cue so the pool table is now operational again.

'Next, for the school holiday fortnight there'll be a bit of extra coming and going with people on home visits at different times, so I want you all to remember to let us know when you're going out or coming in. And on that note, I want to invite Malkie and Alex to give an account of themselves for their escapade during the week.'

Malkie looked bored, Alex defiant. Malkie spoke first. 'We hitched a ride in a social worker's car and went to Edinburgh. We stayed away overnight. We took silly risks and now we're being punished. Will that do?'

Colin wasn't amused at Malkie's attitude. 'You took a younger child with you and are lucky you didn't come to any harm. It was very irresponsible. You should know better, especially with your school grades.'

Alex found this too harsh. 'It was my idea,' he said. 'I had to run away because I was being bullied here.' Everyone looked a bit taken aback at that; no-one ever mentioned the B word. Alex looked at Colin. 'You should have stopped the bullying. You should have sorted things so that kids don't get bullied.' Then he looked at Scipio. 'And you shouldn't pick on kids who are smaller than you are and who are new to this place. It's very cowardly.'

There was a shocked silence and everyone stared, open-mouthed. Alex continued. 'I had to prove I'm not a cannibal, and now that I've done it, I realise it's obvious, and I should never have worried about it in the first place.

'And one last thing. My social worker has got me a place with foster carers near to where my mother's in hospital, where I was meant to be going when I came here at first. I'm leaving on Monday morning. I want to say that if it hadn't been for Malkie I'd have been completely miserable here, and I hope you all feel bad about that, because believe me, you made me feel very bad. Malkie has been a brilliant friend to me, and I'll really miss him.

'So that's it. If any of you have any decency, you'll give me an apology.' Alex's face was scarlet as he finished, and his breath was coming in jerks; but he held his head high. He stared right at Scipio who looked astonished. Then everyone in the room was looking at Scipio. Scipio coughed. The silence continued and Scipio looked down;but every time he looked back up, Alex was still staring at him, and so was everybody else.

'It was just a joke.' More silence, more stares. 'Surely you can take a joke?' Alex glared at him. Scipio looked round; no-one was backing him up. 'All right, I suppose I did go on a bit... I'm... I'm sorry, okay?'

And round the circle they went, each one apologising sincerely to Alex and wishing him well. When it came to Colin's turn, he said 'okay Alex, I accept what you're saying and I'm sorry we haven't been able to nip bullying in the bud here. Maybe we didn't try hard enough. But this is a good start. Let's work out a way we can all live better together from now on. I'll make this a personal commitment.'

There was a silence, and everyone looked at Alex; he realised he was expected to say something. What to say? He looked around, broke into a smile, punched the air and shouted, '*I am not a cannibal!*'

READERS' NOTES

Children's Panels are a sort of family court system used in Scotland. The person in charge is the Reporter to the Children's Panel. If a child (under 16) is in trouble of any kind, the Reporter has to decide whether the child is at risk in any way. If this is the case, the Reporter might call a Children's Hearing so that he or she can find out more. The social work service will also be asked for a report; this means that the child and his or her parents will be visited at home before the Hearing. At the Hearing, a panel of three trained volunteers, who will have read the social worker's report, will ask the child and parents to join in a discussion about what has been going wrong. If at the end of all this they think the child needs extra care, they may make an order requiring the local authority to look after the child for a period of time. Being looked after by the local authority might just mean having a social worker visit you at home on a regular basis but it could also mean going to live with *foster carers* or in a sort of *children's home*. The reasons why children might end up being looked after by the local authority vary – it might be that their parents aren't caring for them adequately; it might be that they are not attending school regularly; it might be that they are sniffing glue; it might be that they are breaking the law, e.g. by stealing. There is a full list of 'grounds for referral' in the Children (Scotland) Act 1995.

Foster Carers are people who have volunteered to look after other people's children on behalf of the local authority. If someone decides they would like to do this, they have to apply to the social work service where they will be assessed and trained. The assessment is carried out over several visits by a social worker, and other references are also required. The social worker draws all this into a long report. The main things that applicants need, if they want to foster children, is an understanding of the challenges facing some families, so that they do not judge either the child or his/her parents; and a range of good human qualities like kindness and fairness and a sense of humour.

After the report has been written, a panel of experts in child care meet, read the report, and decide whether or not an applicant should be approved as a foster carer. If they are, then they will be asked to take specific children to live with them in their own homes, as and when places are needed. They will be paid a fee for this. It is the policy of most local authorities to place all children under the age of twelve who need to be looked after, with foster carers rather than in children's homes, as this is felt to be better for younger children. However there are not always enough foster carers to go round, so sometimes young children end up in a home – just like Alex.

Bullying happens when weak or insecure people try to bring other people down or intimidate them. It can take a physical or emotional form. It causes misery for the person being bullied, and should never be tolerated. Teachers, parents, and others in authority have a responsibility to stop bullying. The best way to protect yourself against bullying is to remind yourself, and others, that you are just as important and good a person as anyone else – maybe not perfect, but who is? If you find yourself being bullied, find someone you trust and ask them for advice. The bully must not be allowed to get away with it; this will only let them believe that their behaviour is acceptable.

Register House (correctly known as New Register House) is at the east end of Princes Street in Edinburgh, near Waverley Station. This is where all the documents for births, deaths, marriages, divorces and adoptions are kept, for the whole of Scotland. All the records are on microfiche and computer. You can go there and look up your oldest relation's birth certificate; this will give you the names of that person's parents. So then you can look them up, and so on. The further back in time you go, however, the more likely it is that your record might have gone missing for some reason (e.g. fire or flood). Before 1855, records were kept by the Church of Scotland and are known as Old Parish Records; since 1855, this has been the duty of local government. Register House also has copies of the ten-year census reports taken since 1841. These censuses show who was living in each house on the night of the census in question, and provide very interesting reading. Under a confidentiality rule, only those census reports which are over 100 years old may be seen by members of the public; so the most recent available census reports are from 1901. Over recent years, the records held by Register House have become available on the Internet.

Genealogy is the study of ancestry. If you carry out a search of your own family, as described above, you are engaging in genealogy. Some people, like Nettie Logie, are professional genealogists in that they carry out this service for other people, who pay them to do it. Genealogy can be very exciting and as you get more practice at it, you can find out all sorts of fascinating facts about real people living in the past. Sometimes of course you don't get the answer you were looking for; and often you find out something that leaves you with more questions than before you started. You need to keep an open mind. Another excellent source of information, for anyone who wants to get seriously into genealogy, are the records of the Mormon Church, or the Church of Jesus Christ of Latter Day Saints. The Mormons believe that everyone must be baptised in order to enter eternal life; so they trace all people who have died so that they can offer up prayers for their souls. The information that they unearth as they go about their research is painstakingly gathered and organised, and is made available for genealogists to consult.

Propaganda means the zealous spreading of ideas or beliefs or principles. Sometimes in history, false propaganda has been used as a way of undermining the enemy. For instance, in the second world war, German radio stations sent out broadcasts by William Joyce, nicknamed 'Lord Haw Haw' because of his aristosrcratic, nasal drawl. In these broadcasts he talked about how miserable conditions were for the British forces. This was meant to discourage people and make them give in to the enemy. In looking into the 'history' of Sawney Bean, it seems that he did not really exist, but may have been invented by the English for propaganda purposes – to frighten people into believing that the Scots were a savage race! Or perhaps more locally, just to warn people not to travel alone on dark and lonely roads. In those days, most people did not read or write – so stories were very powerful as a means of communication.

Teachers reading this may wish to note that this book dovetails with the Scottish curriculum in

- Environmental Studies
- Personal and Social Health Education
- Philosophy
- Language

Further information on Rooshie-Doo books, and suggestions for their use in schools, can be found on the publisher's website at www.galluspublications.com

If you have enjoyed this book, you may also enjoy…

Reformed! A story of Jenny Geddes by Helen Welsh

Murderers! A story of Burke and Hare by Karen Doherty

Threat! A story of Mary Slessor by Karen Doherty

Accused! A story of Beatrix Laing by Susan Greig